LNR PUBLICATIONS

318 Cooper Road

Marion, N.C. 28752

www.geocities.com/nancynorthrop/

ISBN #0-9627894-5-3

Printed in Korea

CONNIE-THE THREE LEGGED TURTLE

By Nancy Northrop

Illustrated by Jeff Duckworth

This book is dedicated to the memory of my "special" sister Connie Northrop....

FORWARD

The idea for "CONNIE – THE THREE LEGGED TURTLE" came to me in a dream message from my sister. She said that I should write about being handicapped, and within the next hour, the entire story came tumbling out in handwritten notes. The next morning I went up to my office (a remodeled farm house on a hill) and started to put the rough words into the computer. As I went about the task, I kept wondering why I was starting another book as I still had "ELFIS THE EARTHWORM" to sell. Several hours later, however, I stopped for lunch and as I stepped off the porch heading down the hill, what was in my path, but a real live turtle! It wasn't there earlier but was certainly there now looking in my direction. "O.K.", I said out-loud, "I get the message, a book about a turtle will be written". . .

HI. . . my name is CONNIE,

and

I'm a three legged TURTLE. . .

Now, you are probably wondering how I got that way and I could make up some exciting story. . .

but the plain truth is that I was born like that . .

YEP – just hatched right out of the egg with only **three** legs!

I lived in a marsh and I noticed from the very beginning that everyone seemed to be bothered about my **handicap—disability,** and they all usually wandered off and left me behind most of the time. . .

One morning after everyone had left, I started to cry. All of a sudden I heard a different sound moving slowly towards me – *"Who is that?"* I asked, and as I looked closer, I saw someone I had never seen before in my neighborhood. . .

"What is your name and where did you come from," I asked.

"My name is SEAMOOR", was the reply, "and I'm a snail who has just spent all night traveling from the other side of the marsh. I was going to stop here for a rest but don't want to disturb you. By the way, may I ask YOUR name and why you crying on such a beautiful morning?"

I replied that my name was CONNIE and that I don't usually cry but I was so tired of being left behind because I couldn't keep up like everyone else.

"Why, there will always be someone who will call you slow–I should know" replied the snail, *"and say these things to you, but instead of believing them and letting it 'get under your shell' , I want you to promise me something".* . .

"What is it you want me to promise?" I asked.

SEAMOOR replied, *"Each day I want*
you to say to yourself –
> *I WILL DO MY BEST*
> *I WILL DO MY BEST . . .*

Will you make this promise to me so I
can take a nap after my long
journey?" asked the friendly snail.

"I promise, SEAMORE, I promise",
and the next thing I knew, the snail
had closed his eyes and was sound
asleep.

17

In the years that followed I kept my promise to SEAMOOR, and did my best each day. I spent much of my time swimming and as I grew up, I could feel my front two feet getting stronger and **stronger** because they were doing most of the work getting me from place to place. I was becoming a **really fast swimmer** too. .

When I was in the water, **FENTON** was my favorite fish friend....and we would spend lots of time playing hide-and-seek in and around the rocks, seaweed, and other water plants.

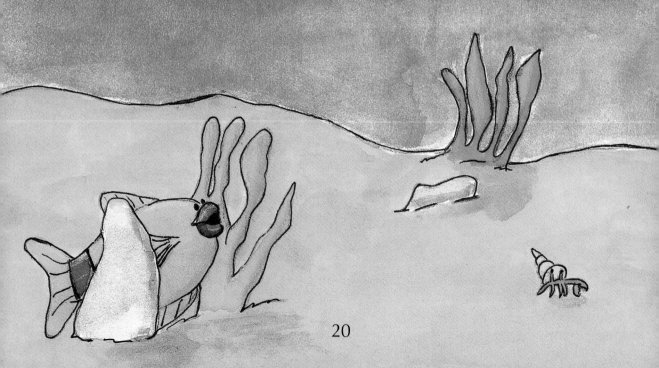

22

When I was on land, I sat watching ants build their ant hills. One particular ant named **ALLICE** became a good friend because she was a really fast worker and could come and visit with me during her break time. We would talk about the goings-on in the neighborhood and watch the other ants working.

One day, however, while FENTON and I were swimming together, we noticed that the water was getting rougher **and rougher** and more difficult to swim in . . .

As I headed up out of the water, the sky was dark, it was very windy and it had started raining really hard. I hadn't been above water for more than a few minutes when I could see ALLICE shouting to me. . .*"HELP US CONNIE, the water is rising and our tunnels are getting flooded out. We will all drown if you can't take us to higher ground."*

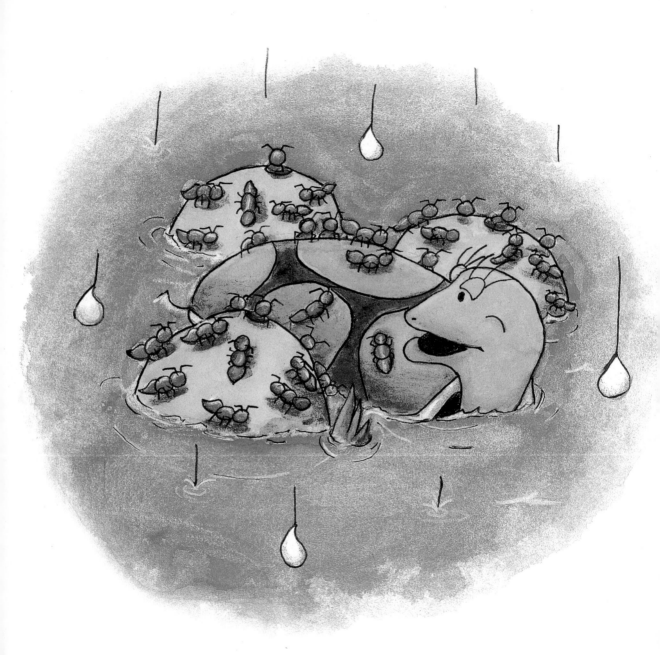

I remembered the promise I had made to SEAMOOR years ago, (that I would always do my best), and so I scurried to the flooding ant hills and told the ants to get on my back. . .

It took all the strength I had to swim in the rough water while keeping the ants safely on my back. I was so glad I had taken the time to learn how to be a good swimmer.

I then swam to where they could hop off on the sand and run to safety away from the rising water. It seemed like I made a hundred trips, but finally everyone was on dry land.

It had finally stopped raining and I was pretty tired from all that rescue work so I was resting on the sand catching my breath.

Suddenly, I heard loud noises coming from behind the sand dunes and I could see FENTON jumping out of the water to see what was going on. SEAMOOR was coming slowly in my direction saying *"I knew you would do your best – I knew you would do your best"*. . .

When I sat up to get a better look, I saw a huge crowd coming towards me shouting – *"Connie is a hero, Connie is a hero"*. . . Even my parents were yelling and I could tell from the look on their faces that they were proud of me.

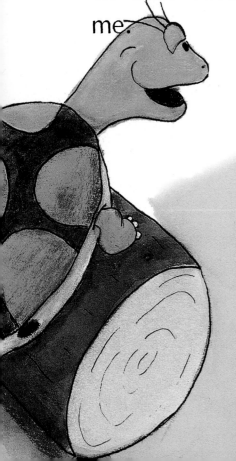

"SPEECH–SPEECH" they all shouted,
"you are brave and strong, and saved
all the ants from drowning. . say
something to us – Connie". . .

Well, that was the easiest and shortest speech in the world to make as I had seen myself in a dream saying these words. . .

"If you take away the words you put before our name. . .

Like handicapped and disabled—which really are the same.

Then look at us again and search for what is good. .

You might just find a "HANDI-ABLE HERO" living in your own neighborhood!

. . . the end of Connie's tale. . .

ACKNOWLEDGEMENTS

Many thanks to the following people who helped launch my sixth book:

- Rev. Adrian who started it all. . .
- The illustrator - JEFF DUCKWORTH - who produced the drawings in a matter of weeks.
- My proof readers/critics: Lydia; Alvina and Ruth;
- Ralph M. Van Dyke of AIPEX-Seattle who patiently waited for my finished work to be sent to him for printing.

But most of all, I couldn't put this book into print unless I thanked all of you who knew and loved Connie Northrop, including the staff at Southbury (Connecticut) Training School, and especially to Lois and Joe for their caring and kindness toward my sister over the years.

OTHER BOOKS BY LNR PUBLICATIONS

ELFIS THE EARTHWORM   ISBN#0-9627894-4-5

WATCH OUT FOR MY NEST   ISBN#0-9627894-3-7

ABC'S FOR THE CHILD WITHIN   (currently out of print)

THE STORY OF MYSTARI   (currently out of print)

LUCAS AND COMPANY   ISBN#0-9627894-0-2